From Epic Fails To Sassy Tales

The Teen Survival Guide

JURISH NATH

An imprint of
Srishti Publishers & Distributors

Srishti Publishers & Distributors

A unit of AJR Publishing LLP

212A, Peacock Lane

Shahpur Jat, New Delhi – 110 049

editorial@srishtipublishers.com

First Published in India by Launchpad,
an imprint of Srishti Publishers & Distributors in 2024

For readers, performers, scholars, and writers.
May my words have an impact, regardless
of scale.

Contents

Foreword

Each of us has a favourite story- maybe a fairytale we read when we were young or the bedtime stories our parents read to us. From the classic to the contemporary, not forgetting the ones that have been screened worldwide on the "silver screen"- these stories have not just shaped our lives in more ways than one but have somehow ignited our imagination and have groomed us to be better people by the moral values they impart.

It's my privilege to present this exciting collection of monologues by Jurish Nath. Apart from being an excellent actor, he proudly adorns the crown for teaching Speech and Drama and Communication Skills for Trinity College London and the University of West London (London College of Music).

I welcome you to be enchanted by characters like Thor, Cinderella, her not-so-wicked step-sister and frustrated Mrs. Claus. These hilarious monologues will give you more than one reason to take centre-stage.

Kudos Jurish- here's to many more to come!!!

I'm honoured to be your teacher and guide!

Kimberly Tracy D'Souza

Vocal Institute of Speech and Drama

Acknowledgments

I am grateful to a large number of people for putting up with my shenanigans:

My family, friends and colleagues for their support and encouragement. Kimberly D'Souza and Vocal Institute of Speech and Drama. My mentors in the sphere of education and the performing arts, both past and present. Shania, for her patience. Benjamin for his critique. Suhail Mathur, one-man army, literary agent, and CEO of The Book Bakers. This book would not be possible without his guidance.

I would also like to thank Srishti Publishers and Distributors for taking a chance with me, and to all my students for inspiring me every day.

Fairy Tales

Cranky Cinderella

CINDERELLA: I've had it up to here with my family. All they want to do is go to fancy parties and pretend we're someone else. My stepsisters think *I'm* the crazy one for just wanting to stay in and read a book with some hot cocoa. I wish I could run away more often, but my Fairy Godmother is a little busy looking for her wand. It's been a few weeks now. She should just buy a new one.

What's more annoying is how much my stepsisters *obsess* over Prince Charming. He's not thinking about *you;* doesn't seem very quid pro quo to me. They talk about every aspect of his life—what he wore to the ball, where he went for the summer, or where he left some glass slippers or something. His name comes up so much in this household, I'd half expect him to be doing all the chores here instead of me.

I'm going to be honest with you. I don't have time for glass slippers. That just sounds like a dreadful accident waiting to happen. Glass is sharp when it breaks, and I'm sure everyone's toes would look really funny all bunched up in a transparent shoe. I don't think I'd want anyone looking at my feet when they look like this (*puffs up face and blows up cheeks*).

Know what I want? *Jordans!* The best basketball shoes a girl could own. I could beat my stepmother *and* my stepsisters with one hand tied behind my back. Do you know how long I've trained to do that? My stepsisters say I'm "naturally gifted". Please. Skill takes practice, and I didn't waste my time fawning over a celebrity. I worked on myself. Prince Charming wouldn't stand a chance if he tried to challenge me to a one-on-one!

Prince Charming: Charmed

PRINCE CHARMING: You know how the life of a celebrity is. Always being followed. The paparazzi stick closer to you than your own shadow. You can't have a meal in peace, and everyone wants to know what you're doing at all times. I'd like a little privacy! I'm still human after all. I could sneeze and half the palace would barge in through my door with cold medicine, antihistamines, and even snake venom! No, thank you. It's like Freud once said, "Sometimes a sneeze is just a sneeze".

I needed to get away from all the oversight here, so I disguised myself as the cook's son, and I ran as far as I could towards the suburbs. I'm so glad nobody recognized me, because I think I saw the most amazing person I have ever met. Well, I haven't really met her yet, but I will. I just didn't want to blow my cover. It's not because I'm shy. And it most definitely has nothing to do with the fact that she was wearing a basketball jersey that said "Down with the Monarchy".

The kids at the court call her Cinderella, but she likes to go by Cindy. I would hazard a guess saying she's a nice person, but if you saw her obliterate everyone on that court, you would cower in fear too! I saw her shoot three consecutive three-pointers in two minutes! With one arm behind her back! I knew I wouldn't find the love of my life through *a ball*. I would find her by *playing ball!* I just need to start practising if I stand any chance at getting her attention. I can only imagine the headlines if I make a fool of myself. "Prince Charming – as good-looking as he is bad at basketball". That's not so bad, actually. It would be a lot better than when that person impersonated me and ran around with someone's slippers.

Anastasia – the Stepsister

ANASTASIA: Okay, who said that all stepsisters have to be ugly and horrid? Do you have any idea what an insulting stereotype that is? Every time I tell people I'm Cinderella's stepsister, they look at me like I'm a criminal! I've been nothing but nice to her. I invite her to go out with me whenever I go out to meet my friends, but all she wants to do is play basketball. I'm okay with that; everybody has hobbies, but I've done all I can to keep her happy. Last week, I asked her if she'd like to go skiing with me, but she said she had a one-on-one match with Prince Charming. Okay, Cindy. Go and have fun, but I'm allowed to have a life too! I don't want to be cooped up in the house like Rapunzel. I want to go out, see the world, listen to all the stories from different lands and eat lots of chocolate.

I think Cindy would benefit from that as well. She would have so many new experiences with me, but I can't seem to stop her from thinking all I like to do is go out to parties. I don't like parties! Loud noises, smelly crowds, bright flashing lights? Ew. That's a recipe for a migraine right there. Do you know what I would like? Camping in the woods. Spending my time in nature. Sleeping in a hammock under some trees. Wouldn't that be splendid?

Here's an idea…

What if I took Cindy camping with my friends tomorrow? We can build a fire, make some smores, and set up a tent. We'll have a wonderful time! I can even invite Frankenstein! I'll just tell her I have tickets to a basketball game and trick her into joining me for a walk in the forest. By the time she realises what I'm up to, it'll be too late and she'll have to help me set up camp! I just hope she doesn't make me do all the work!

Am I a bad person for doing this? No! I'm empowering her!

Cinderallaaaa!

Rapunzel Stays Indoors

RAPUNZEL: The entire world seems to think that I need rescuing. Just because I'm in this tower, doesn't mean I don't like being here! My parents put me here for a reason- I fall sick easily. It's called a compromised immune system. That means my body doesn't know how to fight germs. That's okay though. I've learned to live with it, and I actually enjoy being by myself. I get to knit, draw, and read so many books because of all the free time I have. I tried online school for a while, but I'd much rather just learn from books the old-fashioned way.

A lot of people ask, "Rapunzel, don't you get lonely?"

Not really, no. I have some friends who visit from time to time, and I have so many storybooks to keep me company. Most of the time, you'll find me daydreaming about all the different worlds that these books transport me to.

I also have everything I need here. Good internet, Amazon

deliveries, and a fully stocked kitchen. There's an app for everything I need. Music, entertainment, video games; I have it all.

What I definitely don't need, is a germ-infested person using my hair as to climb in through the window! I think that's really unhygienic. Hey mister! Did you at least wash your hands before you came in? Have you ever used sanitiser?

I was on a call with Cinderella the other day, and she said that I should hire a fairy godmother. Is there an app for that? I need better security in here. Let me see…

(*Dials phone number*)

Hello? Fairy Godmother Services? I need some help. What? You've lost your wand? Why don't you just buy a new one? There's an app for that, you know.

Barbie: Lost in the Forest

BARBIE: Today is turning out to be a horrible day! I went out hiking with Ken, and he told me to follow the map. I didn't know how to tell him I didn't know how to read a map. So I took my phone out and tried to ask Siri what to do. She said "No Signal". I thought she was my friend, but she's been pretty useless this entire trip! That's all she says to me now. I don't know what it means! So we pretended to know our way through the forest when I eventually caved and asked Ken to read the map. Forget navigating, he told me he could barely read! This is what gives models a terrible reputation. I asked him why he didn't learn to read and he looked at me and said, "Education is important, but good looks are importanter." I suppose he's right. In hindsight, it explains why he would never text me and would prefer to send voice notes.

Now, he's gone to fetch some sticks to build a fire. Problem is, we don't know how to start one! I hope he doesn't wander too far.

They shot Jurassic Park here, and I'm scared of dinosaurs. To top things off, I just dropped my phone, too. I sent Ken a screenshot asking him if he knows how to fix the crack on my screen. He said he can't do it. He's such a dummy.

Why are forests so icky? There's so much dirt everywhere. Don't people have vacuum cleaners? I thought there would be more sockets to charge my phone, too. I've checked in all the trees, but I can't find any. I hope Ken comes back faster. I don't want to be alone in the forest anymore. He said he has an identical twin who is a forest ranger. Maybe he's on his way to help us. Hmm... I wonder what he looks like.

Folklore

Mrs Claus: The Brain behind the Brawn

Behind every successful man is a woman, rolling her eyes at him. You've probably heard of my husband, dear old Saint Nick. What you haven't heard about is how *I'm* the person orchestrating his entire operation. Yes, that's right! Do you think a jolly old man who cares about milk and cookies works tirelessly throughout the year to spread joy and cheer? I make sure he stays on track during Christmas and keeps so many little children happy.

Just think about the logistics involved! I have to make sure all the reindeer are in top flying shape and have their clearances from all the countries. I give them their vaccinations so they can travel and keep their stables clean. I even have to make sure the elves don't go on strike. I have to manage about a million elves – making sure they're not overworked, giving them the right training to make the best toys, finding them a place to sleep and making sure the hot chocolate dispensers are always working. Do you know where my husband is right now? I'll tell you where. He's in bed. Fast Asleep. Why do you think he can jiggle his belly like a bowl full of jelly? Because all he does is eat and sleep!

He only has to work one night a year, while I work all three hundred and sixty-five. Just think about the sheer amount of work involved! Two billion children around the world, and I need to make sure that they all have a wonderful and magical Christmas. I really like my job. It makes naughty kids think about what they've done and rewards nice kids for not troubling their parents too much. I just wish I had some help. It can be lonely at the top when all you do is work, work, work.

So today, I'm going to advertise positions for interns. That's right! Human children can come to work at the North Pole and help me with my job. It'll teach you responsibility and what's better, you might even learn how to make some toys. SO go ahead and send your letters to the North Pole. I'm going to make sure you have the time of your life. Year-round hot chocolate!

Robin Hood: Paradox of Stealing

ROBIN HOOD: You probably know me as the champion of the common man, the protector of the people, the underdog's underdog. I enjoy being those things. People need a good figure to believe in in our little town. We've actually built quite a comfortable life. Picture this: I have my merry band of brothers. We live in the forest, but we go into town when we need to. We have access to fresh food and water, and the biggest, most exciting bit of all; we get to steal from the rich and give to the poor!

It only gets better. We have some more excitement because we keep antagonising this old chap called the Sheriff of Nottingham. I wish I could remember his real name, that just annoys him even more. He chases us around Sherwood forest, and it is like a fun game of hide and seek. When he gets tired and goes away, I sit with Friar Tuck and the rest of the gang, and we share stories. When we're hungry or bored, we practice our archery, and if we get lucky, we can catch a big hog or two to last us the week.

I feel like everything is great here, except for one thing. It's the only thing I stand for. It's quite confusing. I'm supposed to steal from the rich and give to the poor, but last week, I think I went a bit overboard. The gang and I planned an elaborate heist, and stole everything from the rich people except the clothes they had on. We did it in the darkest hour of the night, so when the sun rose, those rich people woke up to empty houses! Now this is where my conundrum begins. I gave all the money to the poor, and overnight, the poor became the rich and the rich became the poor! Now I don't know what to do. Should I steal from the rich who used to be poor and give to the poor who used to be rich? I didn't think this through. My head hurts.

Slumberous Rip Wan Winkle

WINKLE: *(Wakes up from a long slumber, still groggy)* Huh? What? How long was I asleep? Where am I? Let me retrace my steps...

The last thing I remember was looking for an excuse to escape my nagging wife. I told her I was going to go hunt a squirrel. I can't stand the sight of them! Always chattering in the early hours of the morning, when I'm blissfully asleep. Don't they know I cherish every minute I can get? Especially since all I hear is NAG NAG NAG from my dear old Mrs Winkle when I get up. I don't need an earful from those stupid squirrels too!

Think Rip, think. Where are you? Are you hurt? *(Pats his body to check)* I seem unharmed...

(Notices beard) Why is my beard so long? My skin is all wrinkled too. It's almost as if I've woken up in someone else's body. If I didn't know any better, I'd think I was asleep for twenty years or something, *(laughs while looking at his hands).*

I think… Yes… It's all coming back to me now… there was a group of little people playing a game of some sort. They gave me a strange drink, and I don't remember much after that. Why was I so gullible?! I should have known not to accept anything from strangers. That's the first thing Momma told me when I turned 5. Now I feel like a 500-year-old man. *(Looks around)* It seems they've taken all my belongings… *(pats trousers again)* My wallet too! Oh, I'm in so much trouble. I've got to make sure I get back to town again so I can get all my friends to find those stinking dwarves.

Let's try to find a way out of here, Old Man Rip, or your wife will make sure you *never* leave the house again!

Peter Pan - Time to Grow Up

PETER: I'd been having a great time before Wendy came along. The Lost Boys and I would fly with Tink, explore islands, and eat cake for breakfast. Life was *fantastic*. I enjoy being me, and I like that I never have to grow up.

Lately, it hasn't been feeling the same though. Wendy is the first girl to be here, and I don't like it. It changes the whole dynamic of the place. The day she arrived, she started cleaning up my room. I *hated* that. She called it a "mess". It's not a mess! Even if it was a mess, it's *my* mess and I know exactly where everything is. I have a system in place for these things. Paper clip? On the floor next to the bed-bottom right leg. Mug? Hanging on the door handle. Pencil? Under my mattress. She says it's not hygienic and I could fall sick. I *never* fall sick. I'm invincible. All the Lost Boys are.

Then she starts mending our clothes. It's street style! Our clothes are meant to have holes in them. Now I have to wear these weird trousers she stitched. *(walks around awkwardly)*

I don't think she's a bad person. She's just too grown-up for this place. That's the whole point of it all. We don't want to grow up! I think she might have a point, though. Cake gets boring when you eat it every day. Maybe I'll try this whole "growing up" thing that she raves about. I'm sure it'll be easy. I'll go back to her country with her and get a job and prove to her it's not as difficult as she makes it seem.

On the other hand, I'll have to wake up early… and wear a suit. Suits are stuffy. I can barely handle these pants! Know what? I'll try again next year. I have some TV shows to catch up on.

Tinker Bell says Farewell

TINKER BELL: Everyone says I'm jealous of Wendy. I wouldn't say jealous though. It's more that I just don't like her for stealing Peter away. She's filled his head with these strange ideas of being a grown-up. Do you think he'd last a single day as an adult? Forget knotting a tie, he can't even tie his shoelaces! I say this with love, of course. I don't want him to go to a place where he will get into trouble. And if not liking Wendy for taking Peter away from us means I'm jealous, then FINE, I'm jealous.

What will we do without him? He's our leader. Who will step up if we let him leave? I can't handle the lost boys! They're all over the place. Maybe I could say, "No dust for you, until you listen to me." That won't last too long, though. They know everyone on the island. There will be chaos without Peter.

Here's an idea. What if…

I just let Peter go. He'll be miserable if he's forced to grow up. He'll be back in no time. I shouldn't worry. I could just give him some dust so he can fly back when he's given up on being a grown-up. That's the whole reason he came to Neverland!

I'll pack two left shoes, so he's uncomfortable all the time, and put his sword in his bag because he loves to fight. He'll get arrested in no time. I'll put some itching powder on his shirt. That should make him cranky enough to come back and promise never to return. Time to commence operation "Hello Peter, Goodbye Wendy."

Nana the Newfoundland Dog

I think I'm pretty good at my job. I take care of Wendy and her brothers better than a nanny would. Do you know why that's impressive? Because I'm a dog! I keep them safe from danger because of my heightened senses. I catch them before they fall, make sure they eat on time, and even wake them up and make their beds. It's like I was made for this job.

But I think it's time for me to take a break. I've been doing this for about 7 years now. Do you know how much that is in dog years? Almost half a century! I think it's time to retire. Live that comfortable life. For once, it would be nice to be taken care of. I could go and sit in the garden, and not worry about someone falling, or if Peter Pan is back. I don't have to deal with flying insects like Tinker Bell. Do you know I almost ate her the last time we were in Neverland? I was running really fast, and I did not know that she was in front of me. Then I heard some squealing from my teeth and realised she was hanging on for dear life. She can be quite annoying,

Anyway, back to retirement. I want to lie down at the beach, play with the sand, go for a swim, and drink from some coconuts. I think I've earned this break. Maybe I could even backpack across Europe! Anything is possible when you're a resourceful dog! I should pack some bones for the trip. Goodbye, Darling Family!

Captain Hook - Covert Operation

HOOK: That boy Peter has been quite annoying lately. Just yesterday, he and his gang of ruffians attacked my ship and left everything in shambles. Do you know how expensive ship maintenance is? The crew and I have been up all night trying to figure out how to fix our sails. That scoundrel doesn't even have a ship. It's so FRUSTRATING trying to deal with him! I don't even remember what I did to make him pick on me so much. Oh, wait, I think it was because I told him that pineapple doesn't belong on pizza. Which is a universal truth! Who puts fruit on pizza?! A crazy person, that's who.

Ever since then, we've had trouble with him. I think it's because he's bored. There honestly isn't all that much to do in Neverland. You have to keep yourself occupied with productive things; that's why I got a ship and a crew. We have a great time when Peter isn't around. I've tried everything to get him to leave us alone. I sat him down one day and said, "Peter, you can put whatever you want on your pizza. Just leave me be." The next day, I woke up to find he replaced all our milk with orange juice! Do you know what cereal tastes like with orange juice? LIKE AN ABOMINATION. He also put toothpaste in all our Oreos!

I try to look on the bright side. None of my men have bad breath anymore, and he accidentally cured all cases of scurvy on board, but I can't live like this anymore. What were we supposed to dip our Oreos in?

The truth is, I've been going easy on him. He doesn't know what the crew and I are capable of. That's why I've decided to show him. We kidnapped Tinker Bell early this morning. We're going to use her fairy dust to fly into their base tonight and steal everything we see. Since they don't have Tinker Bell, they won't be able to fly, and I will keep her hostage until Peter surrenders and promises never to bother me again. By this time tomorrow, I will be the most powerful person in Neverland. MUAHAHAHAA!

Baba Yaga - At Wits End

BABA YAGA: I'm about to lose my job. For centuries, my name has instilled fear in the hearts of young children. You've probably heard people call me other names as well. Bogeyman is the most common one. Ring a bell? A scary man that will steal you away from your home if you're naughty. Just throw you into a sack and eat you up for dinner. If you think about it, I'm like an evil version of Santa Claus. I come down your chimney with a magical bag that can contain many children. I'm definitely not jolly, and instead of leaving with toys, I leave with the kids!

Who am I kidding? All of this was just to scare naughty children into being good. I don't eat children, I'm vegan. I don't even steal younglings anymore because kidnapping is frowned upon these days. All I do is look menacing so children will behave themselves. That doesn't work anymore. I can't seem to do anything to scare children anymore. Nothing frightens them. That's why I might lose my job. I go into a house, and I go BOOO! The kids just look up at me and then back at their phones or tablets. It's like all screens make them immune to fear.

I've tried, yelling, screaming, and stomping at their doors. They just get up and slam the door in my face! Do you know how disrespectful that is? I'm the Bogeyman! That used to mean something back in the day. Now I'm like a relic of the past. I held a meeting with the other monsters, and they said the same thing. Children don't care about us anymore. That's why we've come up with a plan. We're going to start pulling the plug on their Wi-Fi. No internet seems to be the worst thing that could happen to a child today. I'm so excited to be back in business!

Bambi - Adolescent Angst

BAMBI: Life was great when I was small. I was treated well by all the other animals in the forest. Now? Not so much. Think about it – do you know anybody named Bambi? Didn't think so. It was cute when I was younger, but as a teenager, my name is the easiest way to get made fun of. Even the mountain lions don't bother eating me because they're too busy making jokes at my expense. Why did my parents have to name me Bambi? I could have settled for a stereotypical name like 'Roger' or 'Nick'. But 'Bambi'? It's like the opposite of winning the lottery.

All the other deer roll their eyes at me when I walk past. I'm assuming it's because of my name, though my aunts and uncles say it's because I'ma teenager going through a "phase". They're not wrong. The phase is called "I HATE MY NAME"! The only person who doesn't make fun of me is my grandmother, but she can't see very well.

How am I going to make friends? I am going through the prime of my life, but I have nobody to spend it with. I guess I have two options now: I can try to change my name legally, or move to another forest. Both options are rather annoying. If I apply to change my name, I have to think of a new one. It's not so simple. What should I call myself? Do I want a middle name? Do I want my mother's maiden name or my father's last name? Should I just create my own last name? What about Schwarzenegger? But I don't know how to spell that!

Now, if I move to another place, it would be rather tough to fit in again. What's worse is… I won't know what to say when they ask me my name! It's the same dilemma all over again. I hate being a teenager.

Gulliver the Great

Well Hello! Welcome to Liliput! A strange little land where you and I are the only normal-sized people around. Everyone else is somewhat... vertically challenged. When I got here, I thought I would be quite miserable, since they have a unique way of life, and I can be quite clumsy. I almost tripped and crushed someone's entire house the other day. It took me forever to make it up to the poor Robinsons.

Anyhoo, that is why I try to avoid large gatherings, and I try not to move out of my space. It's not all bad though! I helped the King out with a favour, and they've practically been *worshipping* me since. *Gulliver the Great* is what they call me now. They fetch me whatever I want, and let me tell you, if you have a bad back (*holds back and winces*) and you drop something, you're going to want a little helper or two to fetch it for you.

It doesn't end there! It gets better. I never have to thread a needle anymore, they can stick their entire arm through the head.

They wash my clothes, read to me from their books, and play their musical instruments for me when I'm bored. I never got this kind of treatment in England.

The only thing I feel bad about is that I eat a lot compared to them. Sometimes I worry I might be eating all their food, and they don't want to say anything to me because I'm their guest. I've heard of another land far away where all the people are gigantic. Maybe I could take a trip there and see what kind of food they have in store. Giants would probably eat large amounts. A house-sized pizza? That's like a dream come true!

Goldilocks: Seasoned Burglar

GOLDILOCKS: (*Sneaking into a house*) Okay, I've been doing my homework on this place. It's been on my list for months. I've already robbed the Piggies. A house of straw has no security, and a house of sticks is just a joke. I needed to be challenged. I've broken into every house in the land. Even the house made of bricks. I won't lie, that one was a bit tricky, because that little piggy had a security camera. Luckily, I was able to convince Wolfie to climb in there through the chimney, which was a great distraction.

These Bears, on the other hand, they have a state-of-the-art security system, so I had to play it safe. I tripped their alarms on purpose. Now, they're going to come in all worried, and I'll have to act like a damsel in distress. Who could harm a poor little girl, all alone and lost in the woods? I shall pretend I'm a helpless child so that they learn to trust me, and before they know it, I will have found out where they keep their golden honey stashed. That stuff sells on the dark web for quite a lot of money. The Bears have guarded the secret to their elixir for centuries now. I could be the first one to crack it. I've looked everywhere, but I can't find their supply. That's not a problem. I was prepared for this.

All I have to do now is wait. Any moment now, they will walk in, and see this place in a mess. I'll act innocent and tell them I have nowhere to go, and they can think we're going to live happily ever after. They won't. I definitely will. I've got to be honest, their porridge was horrible, and their furniture is rather uncomfortable. I found a bed that is just right, though. I can hear their car pulling into the driveway. Time to "settle in" for a nice nap. Early retirement, here I come!

Sherlock is Suspicious

SHERLOCK: (Walks in with slow, careful steps) I usually like to work alone, but this case may require me to swallow my pride and ask for help. So much doesn't make sense here. I received a phone call this morning and a mysterious voice just told me to be here. It just looks like an empty room. What am I supposed to do? Investigate? I'm not a circus monkey, you know. I will not dance at someone's command. (*Yelling*) If you want someone to do your bidding, GET AN ALEXA!

Now, let's see what we've got... (*begins examining the room*) A dusty room, covered in size-8 shoe prints, and *ugh-* a horrible cologne.

Hang on (*sniffs*) I would say, it smells like wet dog and sadness.

Oh, so very sad. Smells a bit like my friend Watson. He hasn't been picking up my calls today. He must be busy. Hmm. I don't see any evidence of a crime being committed; nor do I see anyone in danger. I don't even *see* any sign of danger. This room is so empty, I'm the most dangerous thing in here!

Wait! More dust marks... A sign of a scuffle. Someone has written "HELP" in the dust. I agree. The owner of this flat really needs help to clean this dump. A deep cleaning indeed. It seems there is a dirty handkerchief here, and a few drops of red paint (*sniffs*). It smells metallic. There's part of a name embroidered here, I think (*Reads from handkerchief*) "Property of Dr. Watso". I wonder who 'Watso' is. Can't say I've heard of him. He seems to be very forgetful, leaving his things lying around. This is turning out to be a very strange day. First, my friend Watson doesn't pick up the phone, and now I find some doctor's forgotten property.

This is such a waste of time. I think I'm going to go home and ask Watson if he'd like to play a game of chess. He's probably free now.

The Super Naturals

Vampire Girl - Scary Stalker

I'm going to say it. Vampires are overrated. I'm only telling you this because I don't want you to go through what I went through. In the beginning, all I cared about was finding out more about vampires. Their hidden lives were shrouded in mystery. I thought I'd be on the verge of a breakthrough, but it's quite underwhelming.

Here's what happened: I went to a small town asking around about their local vampire lore, to do some research for my book, when I ran into Eddie. Eddie is sweet, but he's a little too sweet. He lurks about in the shadows in his free time, looking quite sullen. I assume he's bored. I'd be bored too if I was immortal. I simply wouldn't know what to do with myself after a hundred years. I mean, just think about it- everything you want to do: travel, cook, learn an instrument- learn *five* instruments; it would get quite boring once you do everything there is to do. I explained to Eddie that wearing black, being grumpy, and lurking around in alleyways aren't all that special anymore. We just call them Goths.

But here's my problem. Eddie is looking so hard for some sort of meaning in life that he thinks I am the solution to all his problems. He follows me absolutely everywhere I go. I should be scared, I guess, but I'm not his blood type. He can't stand a B positive. He says it tastes too… happy. Whatever that means.

He's been trying to convince me to join the dark side, and become a vampire like him, but the more he tries, the more it just pushes me away! Eddie needs companionship, true. I just don't think I'm the one who can give it to him. I enjoy waking up early in the morning, and feeling sunlight on my face. I would probably burn to a crisp if I became a vampire. I enjoy hiking in the daytime! I like the taste of garlic in my food! So now, I need to figure out how to get out of this stinking town before he finds out. Just remember what I said – vampires are not as cool as you think!

Jake the Werewolf

JAKE: Your Honour, I promise you, this wasn't me. I was in the woods last night, camping. There was a beautiful full moon in the sky and I wanted to get away from the city and spend some time in nature. Look at the case files! Werewolves don't do what you're accusing me of! My biggest offence is stealing dog treats now and then. They taste pretty good, actually. Here, try some. I brought some with me. (*Fumbles in pockets, then pauses*) What? You don't want any? Oh, okay. Your loss.

Yes, back to the matter at hand. I've asked all the werewolves I know. They don't know who did it, but we suspect the Vampires. It's pretty obvious, isn't it? We're being set up! Werewolves don't drink blood! Not even a sip! Our ancestors gave it up years ago! Ever since the invention of chocolate. We're all allergic to chocolate, you see: preying on humans would be a health hazard to us! We're just fun-loving creatures that enjoy a good day out in the sun, playing Ultimate Frisbee.

You can ask the campers I was with last night. I got a case of the Zoomies, and I ran back and forth for five hours. Maybe that annoyed them a little, but I'm sure they will tell you I am very safe to be around. Now if you look at Exhibit A, you see the victim has no bouncy balls or sticks to fetch. No werewolf will be caught in a place with no bouncy balls!

And if you look at Exhibit B, you see the victim is a cat person. There's cat litter on the floor, and a picture of the victim's cat right on that dressing table! Cats are no fun. In fact, they're rather mean. How do you know it wasn't a cat sympathizer trying to frame me? All you have to tie me to the crime is some fur. It was obviously planted there! I shed like a… like a… I can't remember the phrase… (looks stage left and runs) SQUIRREL!

Mermaids vs Sirens

MERMAID: Most people don't seem to know the distinction between Mermaid and Siren, so I'd like to talk about that today. It's simple: Mermaid: Good. Siren: Bad. Okay? Was that so hard? For years, my people have been confused with scary monsters who use their voices to capture sailors lost at sea. Do I look like the kind of person who would do that?

If you ever have difficulty differentiating between us, look at it like this – Sirens have wings. *We* have tails. Scales: Good. Feathers: Bad. Sirens swoop in from the sky, but we're gentle creatures that like to float about in the sea. Typically harmless, in fact, unless you steal too much fish from the oceans. Then boats *do* go missing mysteriously. We have to eat too, you know? Seawater is great for hydration, but we need some macronutrients.

On most days, we eat a little seaweed, strain some algae from the ocean, dust some shell powder on our fish fillets, and maybe have a sea slug for dessert. It's quite healthy. I mean, just *look* at these scales. Aren't they so shiny and sleek? You can have that too. After all, it's the *mermaids* that inspired the pescetarian diet. It's been a hit ever since.

It's actually the sirens who have all this false propaganda saying that fish will make you sick. They're the ones who started that conspiracy because they're jealous of how people love us so much. Newsflash: stop abducting people. I'm sure that's going to tarnish your reputation. They also said that people should avoid fish and only eat chicken. Come on! Who wants to eat a tasteless, flightless, weak, oversized pigeon? Sirens have no taste in good food. If you asked them for the most flavourful food on their island, they'd probably give you plain dough.

If you ever want help at sea, you can always call on the merpeople to assist. We can also keep you safe from the sirens. Just yell "Filet-O-Fish" and we will swim right up!

No Name Monster

MONSTER: What's in a name? A lot, let me tell you. My master created me from all these different body parts and didn't even give me a name! It's so awkward. Everyone calls me Frankenstein instead, and now the name has stuck. "Hey Frankie, how you doin' today?"

"Oh look everyone, it's Frankenstein!"

I look around too, until I realise they're looking at me. I'M NOT FRANKENSTEIN! That's the other guy. He went through all this trouble to make me. The least he could have done was name me. I would have even settled for a number.

To make matters worse, they even started this rumour about me. Started saying I'm scared of fire. What's crazy is, it's true! I didn't even know I was scared of fire until I tried smores. I thought I would prove everyone wrong by sitting at a campfire and putting a marshmallow on a stick, but the stick caught fire, and I panicked.

Now I have a nasty burn on my hands and one of my sleeves is missing. I guess that rumour is going to be around for a while.

Now, whenever I hear fireworks, I hide with the dogs under the table. Not having a name also makes it difficult to fill out forms. I have no legal name. I can't get a driver's license, enrol in school, or even get a job! It's becoming quite existential living like this. I try to ask the important questions in life. Who am I? What am I meant for? How can I know who I am when I don't even know what to call myself? My boss just made me and forgot about me. I thought I could help him out in his lab, learn from him, but he's very secretive. It's almost like he's keeping me in the dark to frustrate me on purpose. Well, whatever it is, it's working, because I feel like I'm ready to SNAP.

Dinner Lovin' Dracula

DRACULA: I developed a love for the culinary arts ever since I became a vampire. Food just tastes so much different now. Of course, drinking blood earns you some rather unpleasant looks in public, so I try to eat food now and then. Cooking is so much fun! When you live forever, you have to find something to keep you passionate about life, and I think that's what cooking does for me. There are so many cuisines! So many styles of cooking. You can bake, sauteé, fry, mash, boil, pickle and so much more! I hope to try every ingredient within this year, so I can make my very own cookbook. "Dracula's Culinary Delights". Do you think anybody would want to buy it?

I could even put in some alternative recipes for people with allergies and food intolerance. Speaking of allergies, I think I need to address the stories you may have heard about my uhm... aversion to garlic. I do, unfortunately, have an unpleasant reaction to it. It makes my throat close up, my eyes swell, and my face puffy. Yes, I'm allergic to garlic. It's such a shame too, because I LOVE garlic. It's such a wonderful ingredient to use! Pasta? Garlic. Bread? Garlic. Curries? GARLIC! You can't escape it! It makes you warm and fuzzy inside, though the doctors warn me that might just be my body reacting to it, but I don't care. I just carry an Epi-Pen with me so that I can avoid the nasty effects, and enjoy more garlic. So, if you see me at a restaurant, looking like I'm struggling to breathe, don't mind me. I'm doing what I love. Now, if you will excuse me, I'm going to make some confit garlic for a grilled cheese sandwich. It's going to be divine!

I think I'd also like to set up a small bakery and call it "Dracula's Desserts".

Mythology

Odin's Son

ODIN: I know I'm becoming an old man, but I can't be the only one who thinks that my son, Thor, is being a bit of a... of a...

Pardon my French, but he's an absolute nincompoop! I figure it can't be easy to live in my shadow, but did he have to be so dumb? All he cares about is war. He loves ale and a good fight. Do you know what I was doing at his age? Reading books! Looking for the meaning of life, the universe, our purpose as gods! I wonder if he's ever even read a book. The other day, I heard him ask his mother if he could eat the chip in his computer.

(Sighs)

My son is dumber than a bowl of noodle soup. I know. It pains me to say it, but if he had to defuse a bomb with just one wire to cut, I'd start praying to myself. I don't know where it went so wrong. I understand we are different people, and we're allowed to like different things, but he's growing up to be the complete opposite of a ruler. How will he run Asgard, when he wears his shirts inside out on most days! He lost his hammer a few days ago, and ruined a whole wedding trying to retrieve it. I've been receiving complaints to this day!

I've tried to be more supportive of him and his interests, but I can't keep sending him to war. It's bad for business. I asked him what he would like to do if he didn't have to fight, and he said he wants to be a social media influencer and upload videos of himself cooking on the internet. That doesn't sound so bad, but I'm worried he might set the kitchen on fire! It took him two hours to make me 2-minute noodles last night. TWO WHOLE HOURS!

(Sniffing)

Do you smell smoke? I smell smoke.

(Exits hurriedly)

Thor Wants More

THOR: I've been getting into more pickles by the day. I need to figure out a way to stay out of trouble. My father says he's pretty disappointed in me for stirring trouble in the entire realm. I'm so glad he hasn't asked around, because it's so much worse in other realms. Yes, I enjoy a pleasant party now and then, but sometimes, I can get carried away when I'm having fun. There's a little world called Midgard not too far from here. I would recommend some amazing things there if you ever visit: Pizza, something called Butter Chicken, Cheesecake, Kimchi… the list could go on… (*stares dreamily*)

One word of advice though – don't go there for a few years. I left a bit of a mess. I lost control of my hammer for a while and that led to a lot of… well, there's no polite way to say this – destruction. I've been banned from entering Midgard for a few centuries. They should be okay in a few years, though I did offer to fix the damage. They just didn't want me around, so I came back here.

While I was feeling bad for what I did in all these realms, I thought to myself… maybe I should try to focus on a hobby. You won't believe what happened next. My stomach grumbled! It's almost as if it was agreeing with me! Isn't that amazing? *(Pats belly)*.

I know what I can do to stay out of trouble now! Everyone used to have such a tough time cooking for me because I eat so much. There was this one time I ate two whole bulls for dinner. My friend didn't like that very much because he only had three. I ate the third one for breakfast the next day. He doesn't talk to me any more. So that settles it. I won't be hungry all the time, because I'll be making all I want to eat! I won't get cranky anymore, and I won't go starting wars with other people. I'll just try to recreate all the beautiful dishes I had on Midgard. Mmm *(Licks lips)*

I think I'll start by making some tacos… and a chocolate cake!

Lady Sif - Worried Wife

When I married Thor, I didn't expect to be doing so much damage control. He doesn't know this, but if he eats too much chocolate, he gets a sugar rush and starts bouncing off the walls! Him and his stupid hammer, too. It can be quite dangerous when that happens, and all of Asgard has to step in to pick up the pieces. You'd think he would be smarter for a person who is a few thousand years old. I've tried talking to him, but he's too busy stuffing his face with chicken and washing it down with Gatorade.

I've tried to tell him he should eat a little healthier. I don't know when he last ate a vegetable. I don't think he even knows what a vegetable is! If he sees something green, he just says "YUCK" and reaches for the doughnuts instead.

"Thor," I tell him. "Eat some broccoli." "Try some spinach."

Do you know what he does? He flies out of the house! It's quite exasperating. I hide the candy around the house, but he manages to sniff it out, anyway. I know we're immortal, but if he keeps this up, he might not be able to prop himself out of bed! He's already as big as a mountain, and he huffs and puffs when he's climbed some stairs.

It's nice that he's going to try his hand at cooking, because I'm exhausted trying to feed an army of one. I don't have any utensils large enough to cook a whole boar! He says he wants to make a chocolate cake today. I'd like to see him try. Does he know how to put the oven on? How much sugar to use? How to make chocolate icing? All I know is, I'm definitely not helping him, and if he succeeds, he can eat that entire cake by himself. Then he'll get a sugar rush and chase Loki across all the realms. Do you know what I'm going to do? I'm going shopping with Freya!

Good luck handling the chaos.

Freya: Goddess of Fun

FREYA: A girl's gotta have some fun now and then! My husband, Odin, is always busy tending to matters in the realm. I barely have *anything* to do while I'm in Asgard. I discovered a wonderful place called Midgard, and I've been sneaking off to that realm while Odin is busy. He recently found out and got quite upset. Says I should have taken him with me. It gets quite boring with him, to be honest. Whenever I travel with him, he goes to dull museums and wastes time talking to leaders and politicians. It's exhausting! It means I can't have any fun and enjoy the best bits of travel. What's the point of travelling if you're stuck in a hotel room all day long?

Since I'm the Goddess of Magic, I've decided to put my skills to good use. I cast a spell on him to put him to sleep, and then I slip out in the quiet of the night. Midgard is absolutely magical! I spend all my time shopping. There are so many fancy stores to choose from-I don't know how to pronounce most of them: Louis Button, Dolce and Banana, Blueberry, Calvin and Hobbes, Lightning McQueen, Valentines, Door, Fender... oh and Saint Lawrence or something like that. I can spend *hours* in a fashion store, looking at boots and dresses and funny hats and such. Do you think Odin will want to sit through that? I didn't think so. He likes to wear the same old clothes every day.

One of my biggest dreams is to have my clothing brand someday. It would be so much fun to design my own clothes and show them off to people. I hope I can do that one day in Asgard, I know it will be quite a success. I just need to do some more research; and by research I mean, it's time to go SHOPPING! The sleeping spell should have kicked in by now. I'm off to Midgard! WOOOHOOOO!

Hercules: Too Strong

HERCULES: I have a slight problem, but it seems to be getting worse as I get older. I know I'm the son of Zeus, but I didn't know what that would entail until my powers kicked in. I'm strong. Really strong. In the beginning, I thought it would be fun to lift enormous boulders above my head and try to impress the people around me, but now I'm getting a little *too* strong.

If I go to meet my friends, and I knock on a door, the whole thing comes crashing down. You see that chair? I don't know how to sit down on it anymore without it shattering into splinters. I went to get my vaccination shot today, or at least, I *tried* to get my vaccination shot. The needles broke before they could pierce my skin. My mother says I don't need to worry about it, since germs probably can't make me sick either, but I'm losing my sanity. Every dinner is ruined because the plates crumble in my hands. I take a bite of food – I accidentally take a bite out of the *spoon!*

They won't let me fight in the arena anymore because it takes too much money to repair it after I'm done. Fights don't feel as fulfilling anymore. I have to hold back so I don't break any bones. I don't know what to do anymore. Nobody told me that being strong would be such a curse.

Maybe I could go dunk myself in the Styx. I got my powers from being dipped in there as a baby. Maybe if I do it again, I could finally be normal! I should probably pack for my journey. Some food, a backpack, some swimming trunks… and then I'll be ready to CANNONBALL.

Persephone: Travel and Tourism

PERSPEPHONE: So there I was, growing and gathering vegetables, when all of a sudden, a huge hole appears in the ground, swallows me up, and transports me to the Underworld. I'm pretty sure 'Alice's Adventures in Wonderland' is based on what happened to me. It's been quite an interesting journey. The Underworld is a mysterious place, and I have had so much fun exploring this realm.

I also met the King of the Underworld during my expeditions. He seems okay. Says his name is Hades. Sounds scary, doesn't it? He's actually a nice guy. He introduced me to the metro system and showed me the cutest little cafes in the area. It's been so much easier getting around now. I even tried this fruit called a pomegranate. It was absolutely scrumptious. Next week, Hades and I are going to see the monsters at Tartarus. He assured me it's going to be perfectly safe because all the creatures there listen to him. I'm so excited! I'm going to take my camera, and make sure I get lots of pictures to show to my sisters back in Olympus.

Speaking of which, it *has* been quite a while since I've been down here. My mother must be very worried that I've been gone for so long. But I've fallen in love with this place! I think I'd like to come here for a few months every year. There's just so much to be discovered. Maybe I should talk to Hades about that. I'm sure he can help me figure out a way to stay here for extended periods of time every year. I could complete all my duties in the springtime and then come down here for a vacation. That sounds marvellous! I should make a list of all my favourite things to do here! (*While exiting*) Hades! Do you have some pen and paper?

Medusa: Bad Hair Day

MEDUSA: I know, I know. I have snakes for hair. They seem to be in a good mood today, so you don't have to worry. It makes life…. interesting for sure. It's actually downright hell, but I'm trying to stay positive about it. That's what my therapist says. Or at least, *used* to say. He's a teeny bit cemented right now, and I doubt he'd want to see me after what happened.

The good news is, the people who turn to stone when I look at them don't stay that way forever. It's temporary. Give it a few weeks, and you'll be back to yourself in no time. I've received some rude messages because of it, but let's look at the bright side: at least it's not an ETERNITY!

Life has always been tough like this. I can't even wear a cap because the snakes don't like it. They wrestle under there until they pop my hat off and then people start marbling over like a scary magic trick. I tried telling them to stop, but they gave me nasty bites instead. Sure, I'm immune to snake venom, but it still hurts. The last time I hugged a person was in 2015 BC!!! It didn't end too well for that person either. I can't chop the little darlings off, they grow almost instantly.

There's only one solution left now. I will have to buy some tranquillizer to put them to sleep. Then I can finally catch up with my friends and brag about this remedy to my sisters. Now where does one find a tranquillizer around here? Could I go to a zoo? A vet? A hospital? Maybe a forest ranger!

Historical

Cleopatra Hates the Patriarchy

CLEOPATRA: I need to have a word with all the historians who *ever* spoke about me. Why are all academics obsessed with beauty? Is that the only thing you could write about me? It's time to dispel a few myths about me so that everyone knows the *real* Cleopatra, so let's talk.

Did you know I studied Math and Science? I know over twelve languages! That's how I became the Queen of Egypt and that's why I *stayed* the Queen of Egypt; despite so many efforts to have away with me. I'm not even Egyptian –I'm actually from Macedonia.

I also happen to be a healer. I have many remedies for multiple illnesses. I even wrote them down… I suppose you could even say that I'm an author as well. I cured dandruff centuries ago, but do I get any credit for it? Nothing!

I brought so many countries together under my rule. My people prospered along the banks of the Nile, and everyone loved me! That's not all, I also love theatre, and I kept all of my subjects entertained. Egypt truly was a great place to be back then. We had people from all over the world coming to see if what they heard about was true – and they left happy; illness and dandruff-free. Some of them even chose to stay and settle. How many people do you know that can brag about that?

And now, for the ultimate piece of the puzzle. Historians say that I let a venomous snake bite me. Why would they want such drama? I'm not a silly girl from Shakespeare's Romeo and Juliet. I just took an early retirement and decided to vacation in the Bahamas. I'm guessing the people I left behind needed to make up a story to explain my absence. I think I did enough for one lifetime. Don't you? Now if you don't mind, I'm going to go back to my tomb. Good Night.

Everyday Mayhem

Teenager in Therapy

MORGAN: Umm, hello? I have an appointment for (*checks watch*) 5pm? Under Mischief Morgan? I was sent here by the Vice-Principal. I've never done this before, so I'm sure there's lots to unpack.

(*Sits on couch or chair*) It started when I was 7. I met Eminem in a parking lot. It wasn't anything shady. I just passed him on the way to the mall. He seems like a decent guy. He wasn't so civil when I told him I'm more of an RnB fan. Ever since then, I named myself Mischief Morgan. It was a tribute to… Sorry, what? That's not how therapy works? So how does it work? What are you writing in that notebook? Am I one of those special kids? I thought you just delve into your past and walk out when your time's up. Okay, how do we begin?

Ah, yes. The reason I'm here. I may or may not have flung a paper ball across the classroom… which triggered a paper ball

"

fight. I felt like the most powerful person in the world for a while. You know, that's how revolutions start. I could be the King of High School if I kept that kind of behaviour up. You're thinking, I probably owe Mrs Keller an apology, but what nobody is talking about is the fact that she joined in! The Vice Principal just happened to walk in when she was restocking her ammunition. Keller threw me under the bus immediately. No regrets, though. It was chaos. Pure, Beautiful Chaos. Why do you look afraid? You think I'm one of those socio farts don't you? Anyway, the only thing that could make this day better is if we get enchiladas for lunch.

…Do you know what's for lunch?

(*Starts becoming more hyperactive, talking faster and animated*)

I wouldn't even mind spaghetti and meatballs. I like to dance like a noodle when I see spaghetti. Do you want to see me do the noodle dance? It always puts me in a better mood, and after Miss Keller's betrayal, I could really use a pick me up.

(Dances)

I feel better now. We should do this therapy thing more often. Same time next week? No? Why? Did I just win therapy? I won therapy, didn't I? Yeah, I did.

Unless… there's levels to this, and I have to go through different therapists until I find the boss therapist and have an epic battle! You're just the mini boss, and I have to keep going till I face off against the Big Bad Evil Guy. Do you accept defeat?

Lovesick

BLAKE: (*Walks in*) It's been a gloomy week, and it's going to be a terrible month. A horrible year, and my life is going to be a disaster forever! I think Hayden wants to break up with me. I haven't received a message in almost two hours. I don't see any reason why someone wouldn't message the love of their life for TWO WHOLE HOURS! Hayden was my life! I remember sitting on the playground watching that sweet smile and sharing ice cream on a hot summer day. Now all I have is an empty spot next to me wherever I go. Everything is ruined and being a teenager sucks!

I reach for a glass of water. I can't. It's too painful. Hayden used to drink water. Everything reminds me of Hayden. I go to take a shower and break down just before I wash my hair. Hair... Hayden had hair! People ask me why I don't laugh anymore. I can't! Do you know who used to laugh? Hayden!

So now I don't sleep. I don't eat. I don't want to leave my room. I don't want to see anyone. I don't want to know if they've seen my unrequited love. Or even worse; if they say those three words to me. "Hayden's. Moved. On." Oh I couldn't bear it. It's possible I saw my Spookums sitting with someone on the school bus. They didn't talk. It was like they didn't know each other, but what if that's what they're doing right now? Getting to know each other, and the entire time, Hayden's forgetting about me.

Wait, my phone's ringing! It's Hayden! It's Hayden!!

(Pantomimes picking up the phone)

Hello? *(sniffs)* Hayden? You were.... sleeping? You fell asleep watching a movie last night? That's great! I'll be right back. I need to eat four burgers and drink a million shakes. What have I been up to? Oh, just a little bit of this, a little bit of that...

So... *(twirls hair)*

When can I see you, my favourite human?

Addicted

CAMERON: *(Gravely)* The first step is admitting you have a problem. I know I do. I've lied to myself long enough. There's been more than one occasion now, where I've lost time: had an entire day passed by and not realised. I could swear I just looked out the window an hour ago, and it was morning. When I came back to reality, it was almost midnight. That's when I decided I needed to get help.

Two days ago.

I happen to glance at myself in the reflection of my laptop screen when it ran out of power. Gaunt, my clothes are all loose, I haven't eaten a nutritious meal in weeks. Junk food packaging sprinkled all over my room. The dark circles, the bloodshot eyes. When did I turn into this? You'd think it started recently. It didn't. I was an early user. An early adopter. I started at the age of 5.

My elder brother downloaded Need for Speed on the very first computer we had. It was all downhill after that. I was addicted.

(Becomes more energetic)

I just can't stop... I. Love. VIDEO GAMES!

I do! I could be stuck on a screen forever. FPS, RPG, MMO, Racing, Strategy, Simulation; I'll play it all. *(crazed look)* I'll play it *all* day. Dopamine hit after dopamine hit. Win after win. And if I lose, I've still got something to prove. It's a vicious cycle. If I win, I need to get that sweet taste of victory again. If I lose, I think "Ah. Finally, a worthy adversary. Our battle will be legendary!"

Look at my fingers twitch. I'm already rearing to go. I can feel time slow down, and my reflexes improve. I'll play on anything. Consoles, computers, portables. That's probably why I should stop. I can feel this addiction wearing me out. I need to see what else life has to offer. I could go for a hike, eat a meal that hasn't been deep fried. Perhaps a one month detox, like how people give up something for Lent. That sounds like a good idea.

Maybe... Just one last game before I pack it all up.

Best Served Cold

AVERY: I'm everyone's best kept secret. If you see me walking down the hallways, you may notice that nobody meets my eyes. There's a reason for that. A very good one too. I like the anonymity. It helps me stay in the shadows and keep to my devices. *Yesss.* My devices. They keep tabs on everyone and everything in this high school. Nothing happens without me knowing about it first. That's why people leave me alone. I know too much.

I mean, look at me. If I looked like this, I would bully myself too. That's why I needed leverage. I wasn't always like this. Someone broke me and caused me to be this way. My villain arc was caused by... well, let's call them Mister and Miss Popular. The "it" couple. They don't come around here anymore. They had to shift schools after I exacted my honey- sweet revenge. Heck, they had to shift to an entirely different state.

Backstory time: It was about 11 months ago. The "it" couple thought they could prey on an innocent classmate, telling me that I'd been picked for the football team. I should have known something was off, but I was just happy to be involved, you know? So there I am, on the benches, when the whistle blows for halftime. I'd be okay with just being a substitute, too. I wouldn't have held it against anyone if I didn't get to play at all, but then they called me to the middle of the field, and announced to the entire stadium, "Avery is today's Jackass." I guess they were trying to set up a tradition of some sort? I hated it. I stood in the middle of that field while everyone jeered and laughed. The coaches, the teachers, the support staff *and* the parents did nothing. NOTHING. I knew I'd never be the same.

That night, I created a back door into everyone's private accounts. Social media, emails, professional networking; you name it; I had it. I found out who orchestrated my humiliation, and mysteriously, some very… sensitive information about Mister and Miss Popular came to light in the school newspaper. It was just signed A at the bottom. Nobody could prove it was me, but that letter would begin to strike fear into the hearts of the entire school. Once a week, for the next two months, information began to find itself in local magazines, newspapers, websites, flyers, the works. I always chose the most embarrassing medium, depending on the crime I uncovered. Whichever would do the most damage…

People lost jobs, positions of influence, social standing, and some even got cancelled into oblivion.

Am I happy? No. Revenge doesn't fix what was done to me, but it sure does make me feel better.

Comfortable

TAYLOR: I'm new here. I moved from the city a few days ago, and this school is kinda strange. It isn't air conditioned like the last one, and my classmates don't have their own sports-cars. Isn't that weird? Now I always thought that I was "comfortable" but everyone here tells me I'm not just rich, but super rich.

I used to think everyone got their lunches prepared by their own personal chefs and flew to New York to get their hair done. Private jet, of course. I always thought commercial was for cattle, but turns out, actual people fly in those! Can you imagine?

On weekends, the chauffeur takes me and my friends out to the lake house, where we sunbathe on the yacht or go fishing. We usually keep some caviar on ice too. I don't like it very much, but my parents insist on having it available at all times, so I treat it as an ornament now.

I realised I was extremely privileged when I visited a friend's apartment, and it was about as big as my closet. Doesn't everyone have a walk-in closet? I was about to ask them if the rest of their house was underground, but I didn't want to be rude.

I thought having the elevator not working in your house was a bad day, because then you have to take the stairs all the way to the fourth floor. I had no idea some people only go on one vacation a year! Some of the people I have met here can fit their entire life in a suitcase. I don't think I could even fit my sock drawer in a suitcase. I suppose I do have a lot. I'm just surprised I'm the only person who lives like this. I wonder how long I could make it if I lived a normal life. I don't think I'd even last a day. We learned about the poverty line in class today, and all you need is about two dollars to be "not poor". Something doesn't add up there. You're telling me people go the whole day with barely enough money to even buy a coffee? Maybe I should get the entire school a Starbucks card on my birthday. Will that fix poverty?

A True Friend

FINLEY: I've had a tough few days in school. Scratch that; it's been more like a few months. Being an introvert subjects you to being ridiculed a lot more than the average student. I get it. I'm not "visible", I'm not active on social media, I'm not following the latest trends or "challenges". That stuff is like currency in High School. The number of followers you have is a "flex". The views you have, make you popular. That's not me. Staying away from that stuff showed me who my true friends were. News flash: It was zero. I've gotta admit I was a little surprised. Not even one? That's okay though. I have a friend now.

I met Stan last year, and we hit it off instantly. He doesn't talk much, I don't talk much. He's skinny and likes the sun, so do I. I like to read while sitting under a tree, and he just does his own thing. It's a good life. I wish he could talk sometimes, but he's even quieter than I am. That's not a deal breaker, though. As long as he doesn't try to become an "influencer". That would make me really sick.

Hanging out with Stanley made me feel better about myself. I did get some judgemental stares when I was spotted in public with him, but I don't care. Stan doesn't talk about me behind my back. He gets along with wildlife enthusiasts, though. Too bad there's not too many of them in this town. Sometimes, I take him to the pet store where I volunteer on weekends, and he's quite the sensation there. The employees love him.

Stanley came all the way from Australia to stay at my home. He is a species of lizard called a Bearded Dragon. They make really great pets and are kinda cute too. I worry sometimes that he's growing a bit too fast, so I sent a blood sample to the local zoo. I've got the results right here, but I've been anxious to open it. I hope he's okay. Okay, let's get this over with.

(Opens envelope)

Stanley. You're okay. It seems you're okay. Your levels are all good. No blood issues. Hang on, though... What's this? Hey Stan, you didn't tell me you're a CROCODILE!

Entrepreneurship for Adolescents

QUINN: I think I've made a breakthrough. For months, I've been working on an invention that could change the future of all students around the world. I've been ruminating on this for a while. Why should I go to college after high school? I'll have to study for another five years, and word around town is, the job market isn't great. I don't like those odds, so I've been studying. Entrepreneurship can help me become rich without wasting the next few years of my life. I've put a lot of work into this, so welcome to my product pitch.

I call it "The Procrastinator". Have you had a million assignments due within twenty-four hours and panicked so much that you decided to clean your room instead? I've got just the product for you. I'd like to introduce an online platform that gets your assignments done for you, so you can procrastinate all you like. You just upload your question, pay me the amount depending on how many words you want, and VOILA! You have a brand new assignment made by me and my team for you to turn in before your deadline. What do you think? There's tons of lazy students out there who would much rather play video games, or go out with their friends, or spend some quality time with their pets, or plan an elaborate scheme of vengeance.

I could do so much with this idea. I could travel the world, and work from anywhere I want, as long as I have a stable internet connection. I could see the Leaning Tower of Pisa, The Swiss Alps, The Bora Bora Islands, and so much more! Imagine that: sitting by the beach, with a cool drink in my hand, running my digital empire. I invite all investments and referrals. This is definitely the next big thing.

Yes, you in the back. You have a question for me? Please go ahead.

A Pyramid Scheme? No, it's not a pyramid scheme. I just get more and more people to sign on with incentives, but I take most of the profits. It's nothing like a pyramid scheme or a Ponzi Scheme. Because, unlike Ponzi, I don't intend to get caught. (*Runs away*).

Harmless

BAILEY: (*screaming*) IT'S BIGFOOT! Nah, just kidding. I have a compulsion of sorts: I need to play at least one prank a day to sleep well at night. Call it doing the Lord's work, or the Devil's. I dunno, it's just fun for me. I think it's the most fulfilling job one could have. Once I graduate, I'm probably going to become a professional prankster. My parents aren't too happy about that, but you only get one life. Shouldn't I get to do what I love?

I have one cardinal rule for executing these operations. Nobody should get hurt. It's a good rule, and it makes sure that people can see the humour in what I do. Not like what happened with Avery during football season. Humiliation is a strict no-no.

One night, I snuck into school with two of my friends and we bubble wrapped the entire school- inside *and* out! Assembly was hilarious. Everyone was sitting in the auditorium, and the chairs kept going *pprt prrt pop pop pop*. We were struggling to keep it together. The teachers hid their faces too, so that's how I know it was good. What they didn't know was that I put aluminum foil *under* the bubble wrap, and under the foil, was *another* layer of bubble wrap!

We've got a camping trip coming up too, and I have so much planned. I'm going to put a ton of salt in the punch, take the filling out of all the Oreos and replace it with mashed potatoes, and when everyone is asleep, I'm going to steal their shoes and take the laces out. I'll leave the laces in one neat pile and the shoes in a not-so-neat pile. It's going to be EPIC! The best part is, I'll have a few toy snakes underneath the pile of laces. I accidentally ordered twenty of them in my excitement, so there's going to be snakes in the washrooms, in the sleeping bags, and underneath the inflatable mattresses, too! To top it all off, I have the emergency sound system rigged to go off at 4 am. It's going to be a loud and annoying car horn. I brought noise canceling headphones, so I'll sleep like a baby.

It's going to be so eventful. I just can't wait. I feel like I've transcended the human experience. This must be what it feels like to be a GOD!

Nothing

PARKER: Look, I know everybody finds something they're good at, or passionate about in high school. I just don't buy into the hype. I think I was born too far into the future. I should have been a medieval farmer or something. I don't like work; I don't like sports; I don't like hobbies; I don't really like anything. Most days, when I have free time, I just sit in bed, or out in the sun. I don't do anything. I don't read; I don't play any instrument. I just like zoning out and doing the absolute bare minimum. It's just how I am (*shrugs*).

A lot of people ask me what I'm going to do when I graduate. Go to college, I guess. I don't think I'll do anything there either. You never know. Maybe I'll find something I like. Join a frat? I don't think so. Just sounds like a lot of work, you know? The party lifestyle? Not for me. Imagine dressing up. Just to go out? Nuh-uh.

I don't like that kind of thing. Having to pretend like you're having fun, staying up late, talking to strangers. I don't like that. I tried that a few weeks ago, snuck out to a college party that my brother was invited to. Everybody is so focused on snack and drinks, there wasn't really any real food to fill my stomach. Excuse me? Where's dinner? Why is the music so loud? Why are people yelling? How about… you turn the music off, and then you don't have to yell over it, and I don't have to nod my head and pretend like I understand what you're saying? Ten on ten would not recommend that again. Never doing that EVER!

We got home at 3 am! Why does everyone say that so proudly? It ate into my do-nothing time! Why would I want to go to school the next day on just four hours of sleep? I know, I know, it's not like I have something to do at school, but I like doing nothing without feeling tired. Know what I mean? I like being fresh and well rested before I start my day of unproductivity. Is that even a word? I don't know; I don't like to read. I like to feel good while I sit and stare into nothingness.

Teacher's Pet

JAMIE: Sure, laugh at me now. You think that phases me? I've been reaping the benefits of being the teacher's pet for years now. I don't need your sympathy or contempt. I found a glitch in the matrix in the fourth grade and I'm going to milk it for all it's worth. Sit down and listen to the process.

Step 1: Create a demand. Help the teacher. You have to go above and beyond to assist the teacher in the classroom, it could be something as small as having an extra pen or a stapler with you when the teacher forgets it, or something big like having a home-made batch of brownies ready on their table at the beginning of the day. It's not the thought that counts, it's the motive behind it. Total control.

Before you know it, you're at Step 2: Create a deficit. The teacher stops showing up to class with her pens and extra stationery. I mean, why would she? You just made life easier for her. She doesn't have to carry all that extra rubbish to class, and more importantly, she doesn't even need to pack a mid-day snack, because you already did, and you left it on her table. You never said it was from you, so she can't say, "I'm not allowed to accept this." Before you know it, you have reached….

Step 3: Create a power imbalance. Whenever the teacher is upset or establishing consequences for the rest of the class, you are magically spared. Extra homework? Not me? Oh, thank you Miss Judy! I knew you'd see that I wasn't involved in the student protest (that I incited)! You just earned yourself some flapjacks that are magically going to be slipped into your handbag before you leave school at the end of the day!

Step 4: Withhold rewards. People can get used to comfort. It's easy to take nice things for granted. Don't like the way she spoke to you? No brownies the next day. Suddenly, your stapler goes missing when she asks for it. Withhold rewards even on days that the teacher hasn't done anything wrong. This will force the teacher to think about what they did and explore ways in which they can make it up to you.

So that's all for How To Be A Teacher's Pet 101. If you're interested, you can sign up for the next class 102, where I talk about advanced manipulation tactics. Learn how you can get the best testimonials to get into whichever university you want.